MACMILLAN CHILDREN'S BOOKS

The Emperor's New Clothes
and other stories

Retold by
Mary Hoffman

Illustrated by
Anna Currey

The Emperor's
New Clothes

There was once an emperor who was very vain. He changed his clothes many times a day—indeed, he had a different suit for every hour. Every room in his palace had a full-length mirror, so that the emperor could check that his hat was on straight and that there were no wrinkles in his clothes.

One day, there came to his court two rogues who were weavers. They let it be known that they could weave a special cloth with this magical property: it could not be seen at all by anyone who was unfit for the job he held or was a simpleton.

The emperor soon got to hear of them and made up his mind to have a new suit of clothes made from this marvellous material. He gave the weavers lots of money and silk and gold thread (which they hid in their rucksacks). The two weavers set up their looms and very carefully pretended to weave the threads into cloth but, in fact, their looms were completely empty.

The emperor wondered how his cloth was coming along, but he didn't want to seem too eager, so he sent his oldest and most trusted minister in his place. The minister came into the weavers' room and watched them moving their hands busily about their looms, but he couldn't see anything there.

"Oh, dear!" he thought. "Whatever can this mean? Surely I am not a simpleton? And as for being unfit for

my job, why, I have served the emperor faithfully for most of my life. What can I tell him about the cloth? I don't want him to know I can't see it."

"What's the matter?" asked one of the weavers. "Don't you like the design?"

"Look," said the other. "Can't you see the zigzags here and the twirly whirly bits there?"

"Of course, of course," said the flustered minister. "It's absolutely charming. I'm sure the emperor will be very pleased."

And he went back to the emperor and described all the zigzags and the twirly whirly bits with great enthusiasm. The next day, the emperor sent another ambassador to the weavers. He had the same problem: he couldn't see a thing. But he wasn't going to let on.

"How do you like the colour?" asked one weaver.

"Lovely, lovely," said the ambassador, clapping his hands and pretending to be very impressed.

"Do you think the purple goes well with the green and gold?" asked the other weaver.

"Quite enchanting," said the ambassador. "I'm sure

the emperor will love it."

And he went back to the emperor and described the purple and gold and green, not to mention the turquoise and orange. The emperor was very impressed. He couldn't wait to see for himself. So, the next day, he went to see the miraculous cloth. As soon as he entered the room, he felt very uncomfortable. Everyone was watching for his reaction. And he couldn't see a thing!

"What's this?" thought the emperor. "Am I a simpleton? Am I unfit to be emperor? We can't have everyone knowing. I must pretend I can see it."

So he praised the weavers for their work—"What fine design, what glorious colours!"—and ordered himself a suit to be made from the cloth. The weavers solemnly took his measurements and said the suit would be ready in the morning.

The emperor gave orders for a grand procession to be held the next day. He would walk through the streets of his city wearing his marvellous new suit, and all his subjects would look at him and be amazed. Word soon travelled through the city about the magic properties of the cloth, and the citizens got up early and lined the route of the procession.

The emperor got up early, too, and waited for the weavers. They had been up all night, with candles burning in their workroom. They pretended to pull the cloth off the loom, to cut it into shape and to sew it, with needles that had no thread in them.

In the morning, they came to the emperor's bed-chamber, which had more mirrors in it than any other room in the palace, carefully holding their arms out in front of them, as if they were carrying something.

"If Your Majesty would be so gracious as to take off your clothes," said one, "we could fit you with your new suit."

"The material is so light," said the other, "that you won't even know you are wearing it."

Then they proceeded to put the imaginary suit on the emperor, adjusting the fit of the imaginary jacket, the fall of the imaginary cloak, buttoning the imaginary trousers and putting the imaginary hat into the emperor's hand.

"How do I look?" asked the emperor, twirling in front of the mirror.

"Magnificent", "handsome", "noble", "truly imperial", they all said.

And so the emperor set out on his procession. Six footmen in livery held a silken canopy over his head as he stepped out into the street. A gasp went up from the people. This is what they were supposed to see: a grand emperor clad in colourful and expensive clothes.

This is what they actually saw:

a rather plump middle-aged man wearing nothing at all.

But they all knew about the magic cloth and what it meant if you couldn't see it. So they clapped and cheered and threw their hats in the air and cried, "Long live the emperor!" and "Three cheers for our elegant and fashionable emperor!"

All except one little boy. He hadn't heard about the magic cloth. He tugged at his mother's sleeve and said in a very loud clear voice, "The emperor's got no clothes on!"

All of a sudden the crowd stopped cheering. The people looked at one another. Then they all started saying it. "The emperor's got no clothes on!", "The emperor's in his

birthday suit!", "Fancy walking down the street undressed!" Even the courtiers started whispering to one another, and the footmen holding the canopy just giggled, until they could hardly hold the poles up. That was when the emperor realised he had been tricked.

But there was nothing he could do except finish his walk through the streets, as naked as the day he was born, and then go back to the palace. The weavers were nowhere to be seen. But, as soon as he got back, the emperor put on his plainest, dullest suit. And he didn't change it again all day. The very next morning he threw out his full-length mirrors.

Dick Whittington

There was once a little boy called Dick Whittington who had a very poor start in life. He lived in a village in England, in the reign of King Edward the Third, where food was scarce. And it became even scarcer for Dick after both his parents died. The little boy was left an orphan and had to beg for food from the villagers.

He grew up a very hungry and skinny child, always dreaming of what it must be like to have a full stomach. Sometimes Dick heard people talk of London, the great city that was the capital of England then, as it is now.

The way they talked made it seem as if everyone in London was a rich lady or gentleman. "The streets are paved with gold there," they said. And that made Dick dream of a grand city with golden pavements where, if you were hungry, you could just break off a bit of gold and take it to the pastry-cook's to exchange for a meat pie.

He determined that the only way to make his fortune was to get to London. One day he saw a wagon, pulled by eight horses with bells on their harness, and he guessed it might be going to London. The wagoner was a kind man and took pity on the ragged boy who wanted to see the big city, so he gave him a lift.

Dick couldn't believe his eyes when he saw London. The buildings were so tall and grand, the streets were full of horses and carriages and there were people absolutely everywhere. Dick had never seen so many people all together.

"But where is the gold?" thought Dick. He searched everywhere, but the roads and pavements seemed made of dirt to him, not of precious gold.

He didn't know how to pay for food and his lodgings were the same dirty streets. He begged for a few pence, but Londoners weren't as kind to a poor ragged boy as the people in his own village, who knew him. So Dick went hungry.

He had nothing to eat for three days, and on the fourth he fainted on the doorstep of a rich merchant. Out of the house came the cook, who was very cross and not at all kind to beggars.

"Be off with you, you lazy lummox!" she shouted at Dick, "or I'll tip the dirty dish-water over you!"

At that moment, Alderman Fitzwarren, the merchant, arrived back at his house and he was a very kind man.

"What's all this?" he asked.

"Please, sir," said Dick. "I have had nothing to eat for a long time and all I ask is a bit of bread."

Mr Fitzwarren looked closely at him. "Why don't you work for your bread, boy?" he asked.

"I am very willing to work," said Dick. "But I don't know anyone in London, nor how to get a job."

"I'll give you a job," said kind Mr Fitzwarren.

And Dick was so pleased that he tried to jump up. But he was so weak that he just fell down.

So Mr Fitzwarren ordered Dick to be taken into the house, bathed in warm water, given warm clothes and fed till he was fit to work.

And when Dick felt strong enough, he was put to work in the kitchen helping the cook. Now, if it hadn't been for this cook, Dick would have been happy indeed. He always had enough to eat now and a roof over his head. And the Alderman's daughter, Alice Fitzwarren, was so pretty and always so nice to him that he might have thought he was in heaven.

But the cook made the kitchen seem anything but heaven. She was always scolding Dick and boxing his ears and threatening him with the ladle. "Idle boy!" she called him, and nothing he could do was right. The other problem he had was that his room up in the attic was full of holes and every night he was plagued by mice and rats running around it and even over his bed.

As soon as he had saved up a penny, he decided to buy a cat. So he got a lovely tabby cat, who was an excellent mouser, and she soon made short work of the mice and rats. Now Dick could sleep peacefully at night, but his days were still made a misery by the cook.

Now, Mr Fitzwarren was about to send one of his ships on a trading voyage, and it was his habit to let all his servants have the opportunity to send out something of their own to sell. He called them all to him and some sent a length of cloth or a waistcoat or even a lace handkerchief, whatever they could spare.

But poor Dick had nothing. Nothing, that is, but his cat. "I could send my cat," he told Mr Fitzwarren, and some of the servants laughed, especially the cook. But Mr Fitzwarren nodded seriously.

"I shall give her to the ship's captain and whatever he sells her for shall be yours."

So Dick was back with the mice and rats by night and the scolding cook by day. And as her temper got worse and his beatings more frequent, he decided he could bear it no longer. He set out back to the countryside early one morning. As day broke, he rested on a stone in a hilly, northern part of the city and looked back over its houses and churches. And at that moment the church bells began to ring and they seemed to say,

"Turn again, Whittington,

Three times Mayor of London!"

Dick was so astonished that he retraced his steps and went back to Mr Fitzwarren's house and put up with the cook and the mice and the rats.

Meanwhile, the merchant's ship had landed on the coast of Barbary, where the king and queen themselves were pleased to see its cargo. The captain was invited to dine with the royal couple and a splendid feast was set out before them. But before they could eat it, the room was overrun by rats who swarmed over the table and helped themselves to whatever they fancied.

The captain remembered Dick Whittington's cat. "I have something on board ship, Your Majesties," he said, "which could rid you of this plague."

And he went back to the ship and fetched the tabby

cat. As soon as she saw the rats, she struggled out of his arms and chased them, killing so many with her strong white teeth that there was soon a neat row of them laid out before the king and queen.

"What an amazing animal!" said the king, who had never seen a cat before. "Can we buy it off you?"

"I'm not sure, my dear," said the queen. "Would it not be too ferocious to keep in the palace?"

"Only to rats and mice, Ma'am," said the captain, lifting the cat and putting her on the queen's lap. The queen was very scared at first, but the cat, tired after her hunting, turned round three times, then curled up in a ball and started to purr.

The queen was then as delighted as the king and they bought all the ship's cargo for twice its proper worth and

then paid the captain the same sum
again for the miraculous cat.

When the captain arrived
at Mr Fitzwarren's house,
the merchant was very
pleased with his
profits. And he

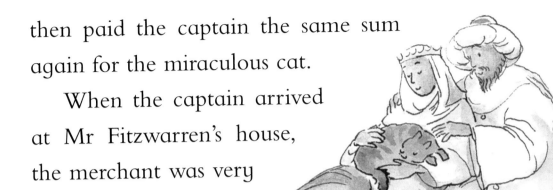

was delighted with the news of Dick's good fortune. Some
of his household tried to persuade him to keep back some
of the money, since Dick was just a simple boy and
wouldn't understand.

But Mr Fitzwarren said, "No, he must have all that he
earned, for he gave up his cat, which was all he had."

And Dick was called from the kitchen and told he
needn't be a servant any more, since he was a rich man
now, all on account of his cat. As time went by, Dick had
new clothes and looked as handsome as any born
gentleman. He had a house of his own and soon asked
Alice Fitzwarren if she would share it as his wife. He
became Sir Richard Whittington and was Mayor of
London three times in his long and happy life. And all
because of a good old tabby cat.

The Three Heads
in the Well

Long ago in England, well before the time of good King Arthur and his knights, there reigned a king in Colchester. He had a lovely queen who died, leaving him the care of their fifteen-year-old daughter. The king was a bit short of money, so he married a rich widow who was very ugly and who had a daughter as unattractive as herself.

Now, the new queen was jealous of the king's pretty daughter and planned to turn him against her. She made up lots of horrid stories about the princess, and she was so successful that the king believed her and told his daughter that she must leave home and go to seek her own fortune in the world.

So off she was sent, with nothing but a canvas sack with some brown bread and hard cheese in it, and a bottle of beer. The young princess said thank you for the food and then travelled along the road till she came to a cave, with an old man sitting outside it.

"Where are you going, pretty maid?" he asked.

"To seek my fortune," said the princess.

"And what is in your bag and bottle?"

"Just bread and cheese and beer," said the princess, "but you are welcome to share it."

So they divided the little picnic and the princess kept her half for later. When the old man had finished eating, he gave the princess a wand and said, "You will soon come to a thorny hedge, but just tap it with this wand and you will pass through safely. Then you will see a well with three golden heads in it. Do whatever they ask you, and you will be rewarded."

The princess thanked him and went on her way. She came to the high thorny hedge and tapped it with the wand. Straightaway,

the hedge parted and she could walk through without a scratch. On the other side was a well.

When the princess approached it, up bobbed a golden head, singing this song:

"Wash me and comb me
And lay me down gently,
Put me on the bank to dry
So I may look pretty
To those who pass by."

The princess was very surprised, but she lifted the head gently out of the well and washed its face carefully and combed its tangled hair with a little silver comb she had brought in her pocket. Then she laid the head down on the grass to dry.

Two more heads popped up, one at a time and sang the same little song. Twice more the princess washed and combed them and, when all three heads lay on the grass, she sat down and ate her lunch.

The three heads talked to one another:
"What shall we give this girl who has been so kind to us?"

The first one said,
"She shall stay as beautiful
as she is today and win the
heart of a great prince."

The second one said,
"She shall have a voice
as sweet as a nightingale's."

And the third said, "She is
the daughter of a king and shall
be a greater ruler than he."

When the princess had finished her food, she said goodbye to the golden heads and went on her way.

Before long,

she met a handsome

young king out riding with his dogs. He fell in love with her beautiful face and kind ways and they were soon married.

The young king discovered that his beautiful wife was the daughter of the King of Colchester and said that they must go and visit him. Imagine how surprised the old king was to see his daughter coming back dressed in silks and lace and wearing expensive jewels!

Her husband told his father-in-law all about the heads in the well and the ugly queen overheard him. "It's not fair how well that girl has done for herself!" she protested. "My daughter must have the same chances."

So she sent for her own daughter and gave her a velvet

bag with roast chicken and sugared almonds and a bottle of sweet wine and sent her out on the same road the other princess had taken.

But this was a very different sort of girl. When she met the old man at the cave, he said, "Where are you going, young woman?" and she replied, "Mind your own business!"

"What have you in your bag and bottle?" asked the old man.

"All manner of good things," said the rude girl, "but you're not getting any."

When she came to the thorny hedge, the girl saw a gap she thought she could climb through. But, as soon as she tried to pass, the hedge closed up and pricked her skin with a thousand thorns.

Once she was through, the girl was bleeding from all her scratches and in a very bad mood, as you may imagine. She flounced over to the well to clean off the blood and saw a golden head sitting in it.

"Wash me and comb me
  And lay me down gently,
  Put me on the bank to dry
  So I may look pretty
  To those who pass by."

sang the head.

"Take that!" said the girl and banged the head with her bottle. The two other heads fared no better. The grumpy girl sat on the grass and ate her delicious lunch. Meanwhile, the heads asked one another, "What shall we do for this horrible girl?"

The first one said, "I'll curse her face with an ugly rash."

The second one said, "I wish her a voice as harsh as a corncrake's."

And the third one said, "I wish her a poor country cobbler for a husband."

When the girl had finished her lunch, she went on her way and reached a village. All the villagers ran screaming when they saw her face all covered with spots and heard her harsh voice. The only person who stayed was the cobbler.

He had recently mended some shoes for a poor hermit, who had paid him with a special ointment to cure skin rashes and a potion to cure a harsh voice. He felt sorry for the girl and asked her who she was.

"I am the King of Colchester's stepdaughter," she said, though by now she wasn't quite as proud as before.

"Then, if I heal your face and your voice," said the cobbler, "will you marry me?"

The girl had been so upset when everyone ran away from her that she said yes.

So she married the cobbler and they went to visit the court at Colchester. The girl's mother was so disgusted that she had married a cobbler that she refused to talk to her, but the king was highly amused. He paid the cobbler a hundred pounds.

So the ugly girl and the cobbler lived together quite comfortably and, if they weren't quite as happy as the pretty girl and her king, they weren't much less so, for the girl had learned her lesson and was a much nicer person than when she met the three heads in the well.